Ten Black Dots
Donald Crews

Greenwillow Books, *An Imprint of* HarperCollins*Publishers*

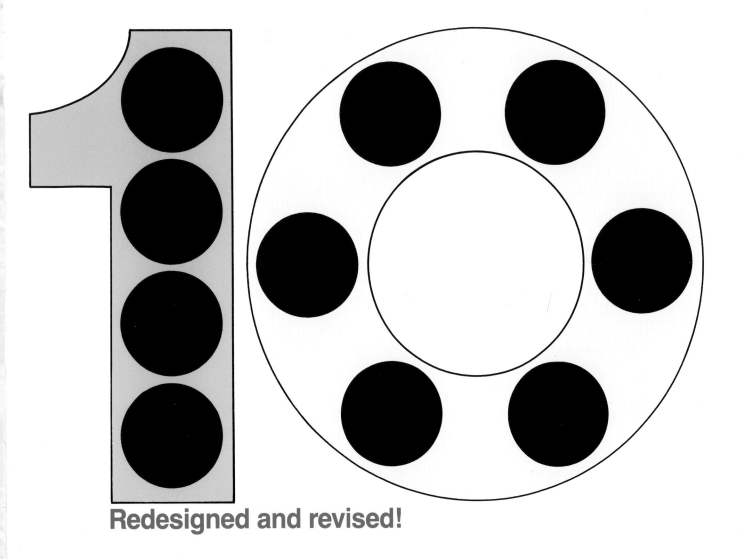

Redesigned and revised!

For Louis
whom I just
met, and
Nina & Amy
whom I've
known a
good while

The four-color preseparated
art was printed in red,
yellow, blue, and black.
The typeface is Helvetica Bold.

Ten Black Dots
Copyright © 1968, 1986
by Donald Crews
All rights reserved.
Printed in the United States of America
For information address
HarperCollins Children's
Books, a division of
HarperCollins Publishers,
195 Broadway,
New York, NY 10007.
www.harperchildrens.com
First Edition
20 21 22 PC
30 29 28 27

Library of Congress
Cataloging-in-Publication Data
Crews, Donald.
Ten black dots.
Summary: A counting book
which shows what can be
done with ten black dots—
one can make a sun,
two a fox's eyes, or
eight the wheels of a train.
[1. Counting.
2. Stories in rhyme]
I. Title
II. Title: 10 black dots
PZ8.3.C867Te 1986
[E]   85-14871
ISBN 0-688-06067-6 (trade)
ISBN 0-688-06068-4 (lib. bdg.)
ISBN 0-688-13574-9 (pbk.)

What can you do with ten black dots?

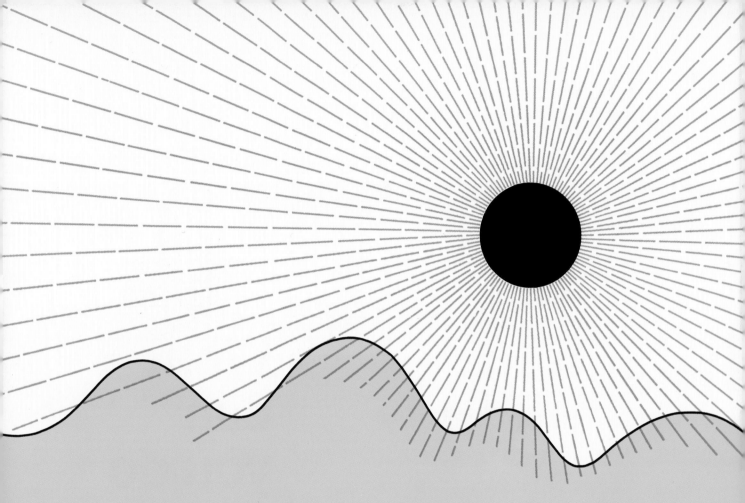

**1 One dot
can make
a sun**

**or a moon
when day
is done.**

2 Two dots
can make the
eyes of a fox

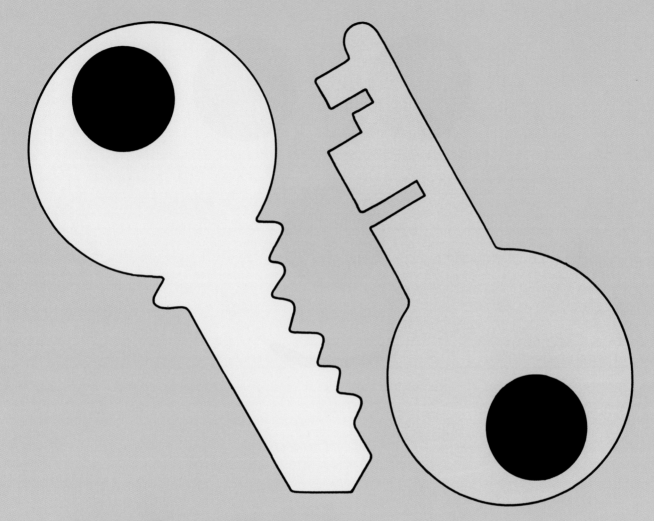

**or the eyes
of keys that
open locks.**

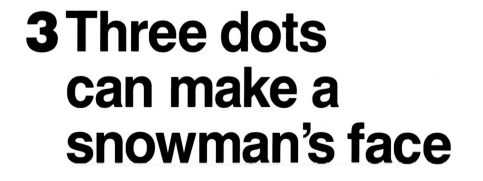

3 Three dots
can make a
snowman's face

**or beads
for stringing
on a lace.**

**4 Four dots
can make seeds from
which flowers grow**

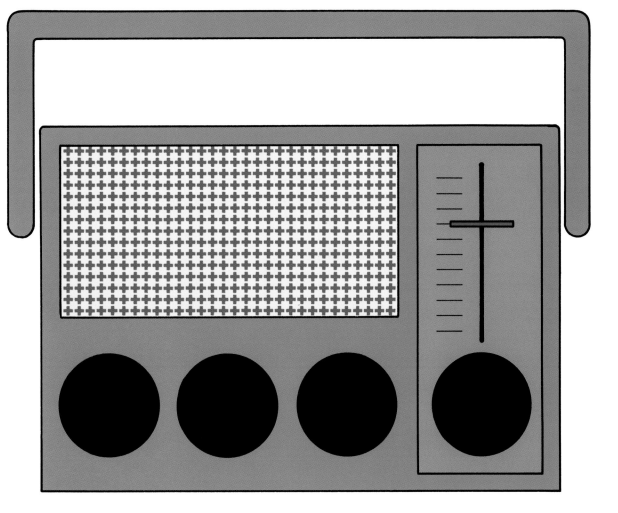

**or the
knobs on
a radio.**

5 Five dots
can make buttons
on a coat

**or the
portholes
of a boat.**

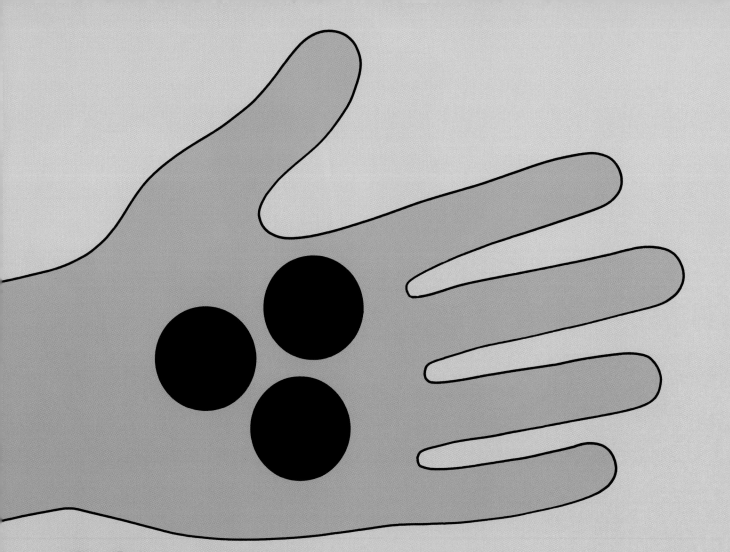

**6 Six dots
can make marbles
that you hold—**

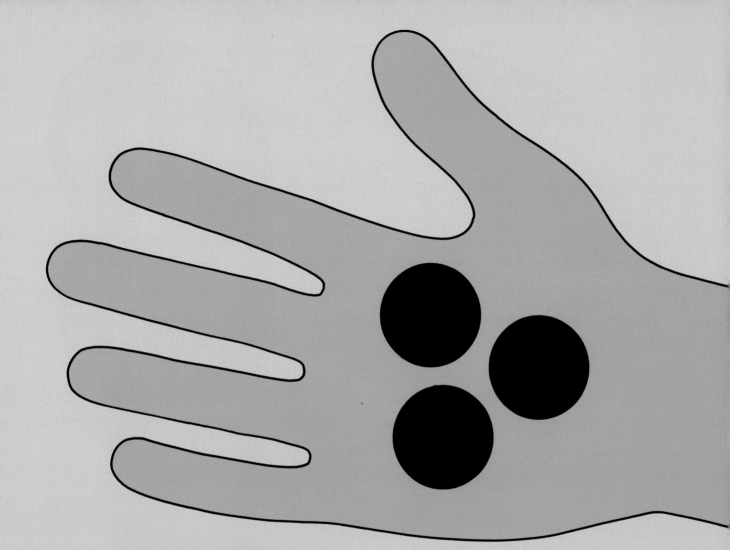

**half are
new, the rest
are old.**

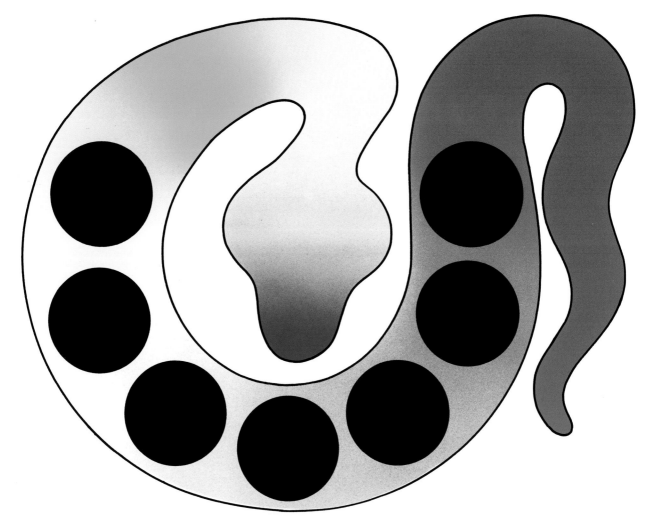

7 **Seven dots**
can make the spots
on a snake

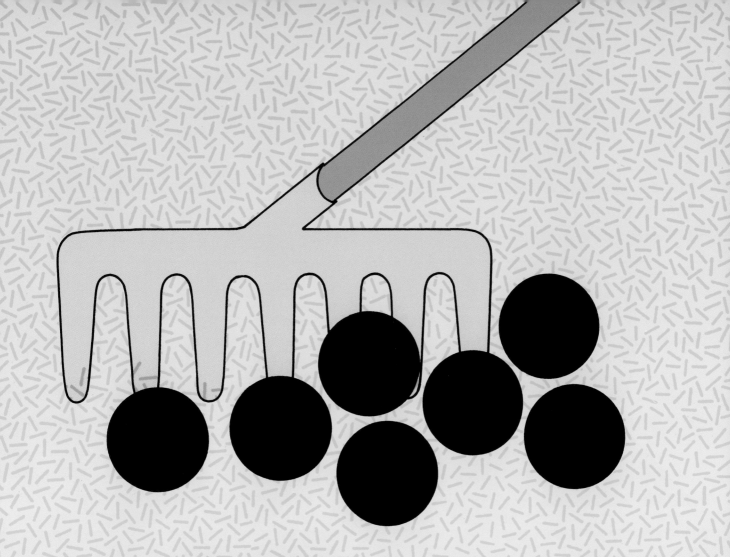

**or stones
turned up by a
garden rake.**

**8 Eight dots
can make the
wheels of a train**

**carrying freight
through sun
and rain.**

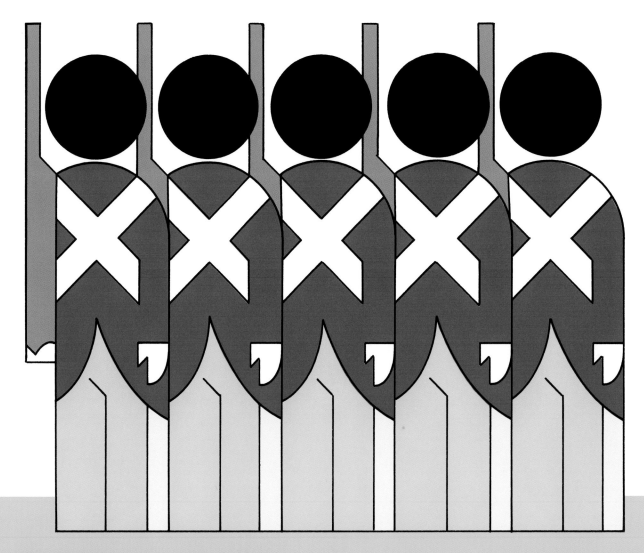

**9 Nine dots
can make toy soldiers
standing in rank**

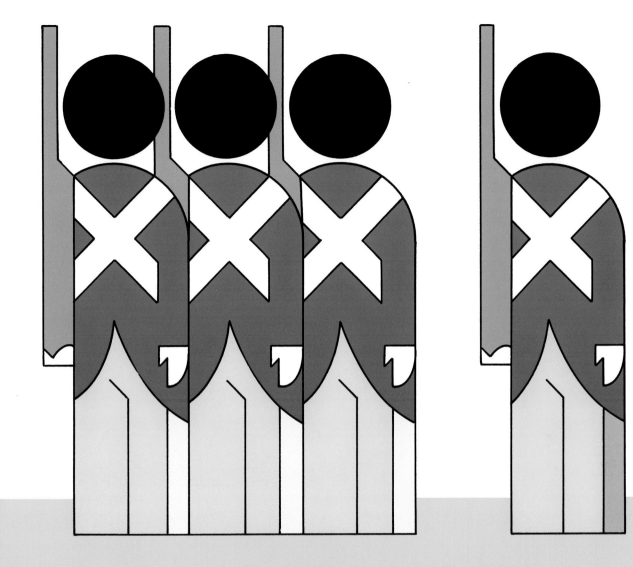

**or the pennies
in your
piggy bank.**

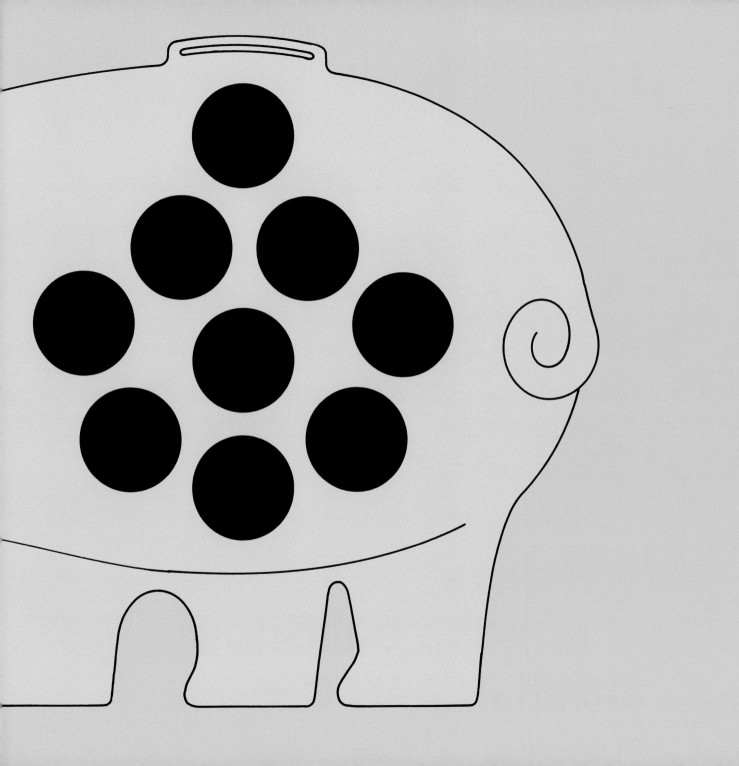

10 Ten dots
can make balloons
stuck in a tree—

**shake the branch
and set
them free.**

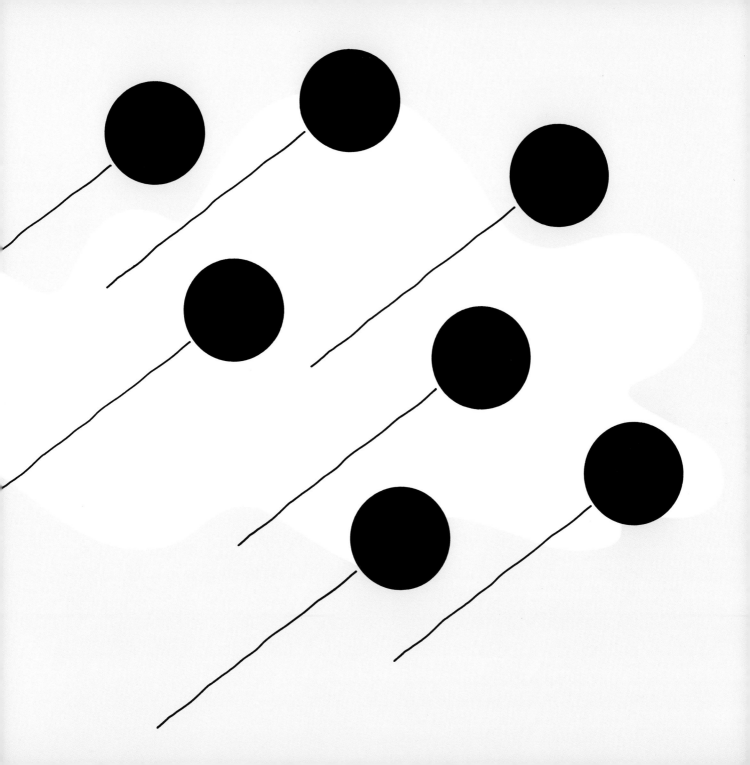

Count
them.
Are there
really ten?
Now we
can begin
again,
counting
dots
from one
to ten.

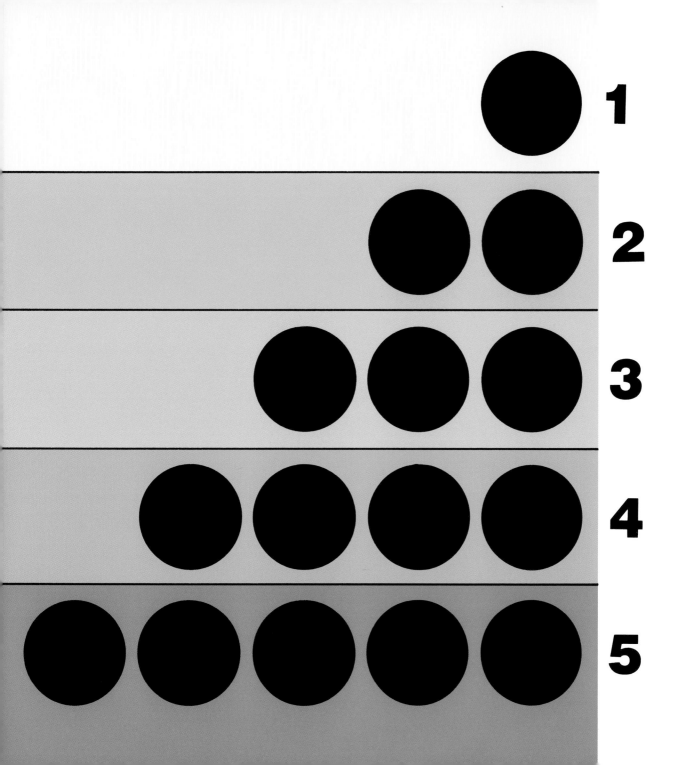

1

2

3

4

5

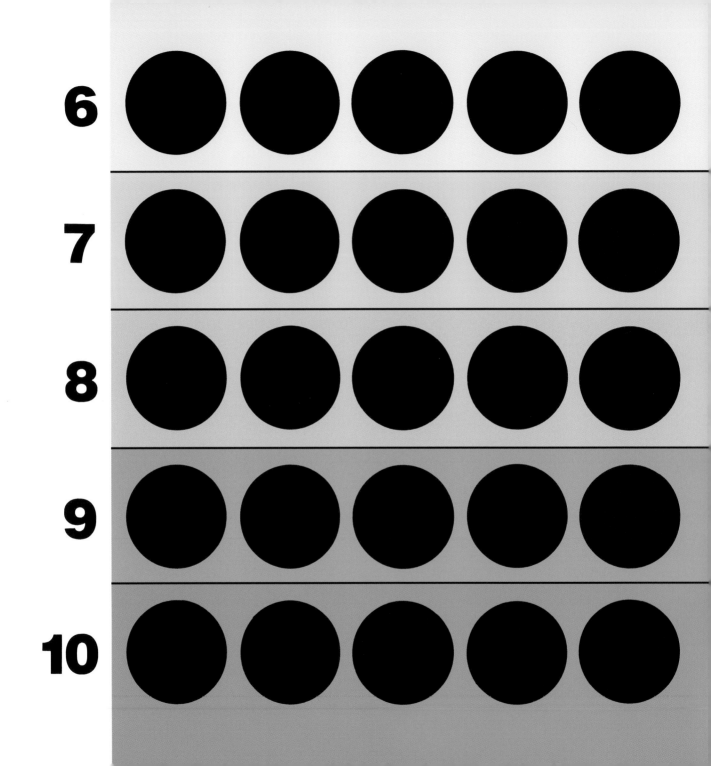